The Big Adventures of
TINY HOUSE

by Susan Schaefer Bernardo   illustrated by Courtenay Fletcher

Inner Flower Child Books

LOS ANGELES

Love and thanks to Los Encinos School, the Miller Family
and all of the people who helped get Tiny rolling on his big adventure.

— xoxo Courtenay & Susan

Text copyright © 2017 by Susan Schaefer Bernardo
Illustrations copyright © 2017 by Courtenay Fletcher

First Edition: April 2017
10 9 8 7 6 5 4 3 2 1
ISBN 978-0-9711228-2-6 (hardcover)

Publisher's Cataloging-In-Publication Data (Prepared by The Donohue Group, Inc.)
Names: Bernardo, Susan Schaefer. | Fletcher, Courtenay, illustrator.
Title: The Big Adventures of Tiny House / by Susan Schaefer Bernardo ; illustrated by Courtenay Fletcher.
Description: First edition. | Los Angeles : Inner Flower Child Books, 2017. | Interest age level: 003-008. | Summary: An old farmhouse gets recycled into something new: Tiny, a little house with a big heart and wheels. With the help of his friend Big Truck, Tiny travels thousands of miles across America. Along the way, he meets cool new friends like Shiny (an Airstream), Waverly (a houseboat) and Buster (a converted school bus). In the end, Tiny realizes that he has exactly what it takes to be a real home.
Identifiers: LCCN 2016921211 | ISBN 978-0-9711228-2-6 (hardcover)
Subjects: LCSH: Small houses--Juvenile fiction. | Mobile homes--Juvenile fiction. | Recycling (Waste, etc.)--Juvenile fiction. | Friendship--Juvenile fiction. | United States--Description and travel--Juvenile fiction. | CYAC: Mobile homes--Fiction. | Recycling (Waste)--Fiction. | Friendship--Fiction. | United States--Description and travel--Fiction. | LCGFT: Picture books. | Stories in rhyme.
Classification: LCC PZ7.B47 Bi 2017 | DDC [E]--dc23

Visit us at www.SunKissesMoonHugs.com & www.TheBigAdventuresofTinyHouse.com

Book design by Courtenay Fletcher
Printed and bound in the USA by Bang Printing.
We love trees. This book was made with recycled paper.

SUSTAINABLE FORESTRY INITIATIVE

Certified Chain of Custody
Promoting Sustainable Forestry
www.sfiprogram.org
SFI-01268

SFI label applies to the text stock

Once there was a farmhouse in a field of hay,

but while it lay sleeping, the acres gave way
to a bustling city whose bright, shiny towers
edged out the farmhouse, the fields and flowers.

FOR
SALE

Clever hands salvaged the windows and doors,
recycled the wood from the walls and the floors.
Hoping to find a more neighborly view,
they picked up those pieces and built something new.

With some nails
and a saw...
and a hammer
with a claw...
they made...

A sweet little house, cozy and snug,
with a tiny front porch and a red braided rug,
a tuck-away table and a neat little nook
for writing a letter or reading a book.

A loft made for sleeping and happy stargazing

and dreams of a life that was big and amazing.

Cabinets crafted from fallen down trees...

and best of all, **wheels**,

so he could go where he pleased.

Though they didn't have room for all their old stuff,
what they decided to keep was exactly enough.

Tiny liked his new shape and his rolling foundation,
but how would he get to his next destination?

Here came Big Truck, sturdy and strong,
with a hitch at her back to tow Tiny along.

That little house on the road caught everyone's eye!
Children waved and blew kisses when Tiny rolled by.

To see the world whizzing past

gave Tiny a thrill...

'til they passed Missy Mansion

where she sat on her hill.

She took a long look

and with scorn on her face,

said, "You can't be a home

if you don't stay in one place."

Tiny was troubled, could that big house be right?
Was he really a home if he wasn't stuck tight?
But he didn't have time to worry too long—
Big Truck was rolling and singing her song.

"The sun's shining bright, and we've got a green light...
Let's drive!"

Driving's just what they did, heading west with the sun,
looking for landmarks and friendship and fun.

In St. Louis they stopped near a remarkable arch.

In New Orleans they joined a parade on the march.

They turned left at Texas and placed a big order for tacos at a stand just south of the border.

With a RATTLE!
and a POP!
Truck rumbled
to a stop.
"Oh, no!"

"My tank's almost empty, and my tires are flat, but I know just the place to fix all of that.
No need to fret or fall into frustration—we can find what we need at Granny's Gas Station."

Granny filled them up with tender loving care—water in the radiator, tires pumped with air.
While Big Truck enjoyed the rest she was taking, Tiny was tickled by the friend he was making!

She was a silvery sort, 'bout the same size as Tiny,
who said with a drawl, "Y'all call me Shiny!"

How fun! What joy! A new traveling companion!
And they rolled down the road to the famous Grand Canyon.

When they drove through the desert,
Tiny got practice
swerving to miss
the sharp spines of a cactus!

Winding up through the Rockies,
they got covered in snow,
so they headed back down
to the valley below.

They stopped at a drawbridge and looked down in wonder
as a strange-looking ship tootled right under.

"Toot! Toot! Splish-Splash!"

"I'm Waverly," he said. "I'm a house on a boat.
I live on this water. See? I can float!"

"A home on the water? Can such a thing be?"

"Of course!" said the houseboat. "Why, look at me!
I've got walls and a roof to keep the rain out.
I'm a wonderful home, even floating about."

Life alone on the road was losing its luster,
when they heard the horn
of a skoolie named Buster.

"Beep! Beep!

Honk! Honk!"

"If you're looking for adventure, just follow me
to the axle-hoppin', wheel-stompin' Tiny House Jamboree.
We'll raise the roof with our ruckus! All our kin will be coming!
There'll be ringing and singing and dancing and drumming!"

Tiny was proud
of this grand celebration,
and his shingles fair shimmered
with joy and elation.
They stayed up 'til midnight
swapping songs and tall tales
of the adventures they'd had
on their tiny house trails.
Tiny talked of his plans
to visit the stars—
how he would hitch to a rocket
and zoom straight to Mars!

When the songs had been sung
and the stories all told,
the jamboree ended,
and they got back on the road.

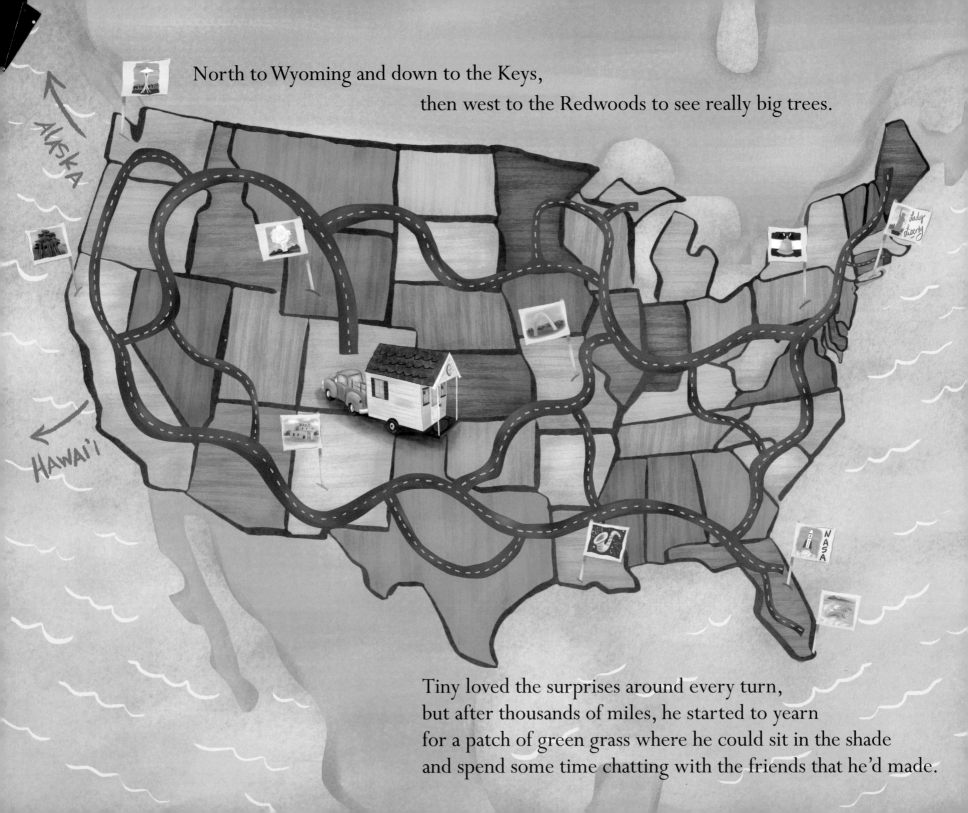

North to Wyoming and down to the Keys,
then west to the Redwoods to see really big trees.

Tiny loved the surprises around every turn,
but after thousands of miles, he started to yearn
for a patch of green grass where he could sit in the shade
and spend some time chatting with the friends that he'd made.

He thought about Missy, up high on her hill.
He hoped she was happy, sitting there still.
As for him, he was looking for a new way of living—
a community founded on sharing and giving.
He found a good spot under an old apple tree
and settled down with his friends in sweet Harmony.

With some nails and a saw...
and a hammer with a claw...
they grew...
something new!

A tiny house village full of chatter and charm with a view of the river and an organic farm.

He could be a home anywhere, because home wasn't a place.
Home was a feeling, a smile on your face.
Home was friendship and singing and a full happy heart—
it was sharing good meals and where you hung up your art.

HARMONY GARDEN

Whether you dropped your anchor
or decided to roam,
what called to your heart
could still be called home.

And when Tiny woke up with that traveling itch...
Big Truck was ready to hook up the hitch.